TEXAS RANGERS

by Ryan Basen

Published by ABDO Publishing Company, 8000 West 78th Street, Edina, Minnesota 55439. Copyright © 2011 by Abdo Consulting Group, Inc. International copyrights reserved in all countries. No part of this book may be reproduced in any form without written permission from the publisher. SportsZone™ is a trademark and logo of ABDO Publishing Company.

Printed in the United States of America,
North Mankato, Minnesota
112010
012011

 THIS BOOK CONTAINS AT LEAST 10% RECYCLED MATERIALS.

Editor: Chrös McDougall
Copy Editor: Nicholas Cafarelli
Interior Design and Production: Kazuko Collins
Cover Design: Kazuko Collins

Photo Credits: Cody Duty/AP Images, cover; Eric Gay/AP Images, 1, 30, 33, 43 (middle); Kyodo via AP Images, 4, 43 (bottom); Chris O'Meara/AP Images, 7; Paul Sancya/AP Images, 9; Tony Gutierrez/AP Images, 11; AP Images, 12, 14, 17, 18, 20, 42 (top and middle); Bill Janscha/AP Images, 22, 28, 35, 42 (bottom); Jim Mone/AP Images, 25; Andy Sharp/AP Images, 27, 43 (top); Reed Saxon/AP Images, 36; Linda Kaye/AP Images, 39; John Raoux/AP Images, 40; Ralph Lauer/AP Images, 44; Julia Robertson/AP Images, 47

Library of Congress Cataloging-in-Publication Data
Basen, Ryan.
  Texas Rangers / by Ryan Basen.
      p. cm. — (Inside MLB)
  Includes index.
  ISBN 978-1-61714-061-7
  1. Texas Rangers (Baseball team)—History—Juvenile literature. I. Title.
  GV875.T4B37 2011
  796.357'6409764531—dc22
                                    2010045322

TABLE OF CONTENTS

Chapter 1 .... Winning the Pennant, 4

Chapter 2 .... Same Old Senators, 12

Chapter 3 .... New Home on the Range, 18

Chapter 4 .... A New Era, 28

Chapter 5 .... A Costly Mistake and a Rebirth, 36

Timeline, 42

Quick Stats, 44

Quotes and Anecdotes, 45

Glossary, 46

For More Information, 47

Index, 48

About the Author, 48

CHAPTER 1

WINNING THE PENNANT

Neftali Feliz had a chance to make history. The Texas Rangers had a 3–2 lead in the 2010 American League (AL) Championship Series. With two outs in the top of the ninth inning of Game 6, the Rangers led the New York Yankees 6–1. Feliz, the Rangers' closer, needed just one more out to send his team to its first World Series.

Yankees star Alex Rodriguez was at the plate. More than 51,000 fans at Rangers Ballpark in Arlington stood and cheered as Feliz got two strikes on Rodriguez. Then he threw an 83-miles-per-hour slider. Rodriguez watched as the ball cut back into the strike zone. The umpire called strike three.

Fans erupted. The Rangers rushed to the mound to celebrate. After half a century—including 39 seasons in Texas—the Rangers were going to the World Series.

Vladimir Guerrero jumps on top of his Rangers teammates in celebration after they defeated the New York Yankees in the 2010 AL Championship Series to advance to the team's first World Series.

WINNING THE PENNANT

"I'm so excited," center fielder Josh Hamilton said. "You know this is something that has never happened here before. To be part of something like that means the world."

The game marked the culmination of the Rangers' breakthrough 2010 season. The franchise had endured a mostly sorry history to that point. Since debuting as the Washington Senators in 1961, the team had never won an AL pennant until 2010. In fact, the Rangers had never even won a playoff series until they beat the Tampa Bay Rays in the 2010 AL Division Series (ALDS).

The foundation for the Rangers' successful season was set the previous year. In 2009, the Rangers posted a winning record for only the second time in 10 years. They played aggressive, fundamental baseball under manager Ron Washington. With standouts such as Feliz, third baseman Michael Young, second baseman Ian Kinsler, and outfielders Hamilton and Nelson Cruz, the Rangers were ready to contend in 2010.

That is exactly what they did. The Rangers took over first place in the AL West Division on June 8. Winning streaks of

Adding an Ace

When the 2010 Seattle Mariners' season turned sour, they decided to trade ace pitcher Cliff Lee. Many thought the free-spending New York Yankees were a likely destination. The surging Minnesota Twins were an option as well. But on July 9, the Mariners sent Lee to the Rangers. The trade sent a message that the Rangers meant business. Lee helped the Rangers win the AL West. Then he won his first three starts in the postseason to help the Rangers secure their first pennant. That included an 8–0 playoff win over the Yankees when the left-hander held New York to two hits and one walk in eight innings.

Cliff Lee pitched the Rangers to a 5–1 victory in Game 1 of the 2010 ALDS against the Tampa Bay Rays.

11 and seven games helped the club increase its division lead to 10 games by mid-September. Then, on September 25, first baseman Jorge Cantu hit an eighth-inning home run that gave the Rangers a 4–3 win over the Oakland Athletics. The victory clinched the Rangers' first AL West title since 1999.

Despite the Rangers' great regular season, few considered them a favorite in the playoffs. Many thought they would lose to the AL East champion Rays in the ALDS. But Rangers ace Cliff Lee shut down the Rays in a 5–1 win in Game 1. C. J. Wilson, Darren O'Day, and Darren Oliver combined to hold

WINNING THE PENNANT **7**

Tampa Bay to two hits in a 6–0 Game 2 victory.

The Rangers faltered when the series returned to Texas for the third and fourth games, losing both. That set up the decisive fifth game in Tampa. But the Rangers won 5–1 behind a complete game from Lee and strong performances from Kinsler and Cruz. It was the first time the Rangers had won a postseason series.

Even fewer people gave the Rangers a shot against the powerful Yankees in the AL Championship Series (ALCS). The Yankees had just dominated the Minnesota Twins in the ALDS. They came out strong with a 6–5 win in Game 1. However, the Rangers came back in Game 2. They exploded for five runs in the first three innings. Starter Colby Lewis held the Yankees to two runs in six innings. The Rangers won 7–2 for the team's first home playoff win ever.

The Rangers continued to roll as the series shifted to New York. Lee shut out the Yankees 8–0 in Game 3. The Rangers smashed 13 hits to win Game 4 by a score of 10–3. After losing Game 5, Texas returned home for Game 6.

With the game tied 1–1 in the fifth, Rangers designated hitter Vladimir Guerrero hit a double to score two runs. Cruz then banged a two-run homer

Young Guns

Two pitchers who were not major league starters in 2009 emerged a year later to give the Rangers a solid rotation. Colby Lewis and C. J. Wilson won a combined 27 games in the regular season. In the playoffs, Wilson won Game 2 over the Rays in the ALDS and Lewis won two games in the ALCS and Game 3 of the World Series. "They've come up huge in every big spot for us," Rangers third baseman Michael Young said.

Third baseman Michael Young, *left*, and second baseman Ian Kinsler provided excellent defense in the Rangers' run to the 2010 World Series.

to left-center to give Texas a 5–1 lead. When Feliz closed out the ninth inning, the Rangers were headed to their first World Series.

The Rangers faced the upstart San Francisco Giants in the World Series. Like the Rangers, the Giants were considered big underdogs to reach the World Series when the season started. But the Giants' pitchers were red hot in the playoffs. The Rangers lost the first two games of the Series in San Francisco. The Rangers did not even score a run in Game 2.

Fans were optimistic as the World Series came to north Texas for the first time for Game 3. The Rangers indeed gave them a treat. Rangers first baseman Mitch Moreland belted a three-run homer while

WINNING THE PENNANT 9

JOSH HAMILTON

Rangers outfielder Josh Hamilton enjoyed an incredible 2008 Home Run Derby. He smashed a record 28 homers in the first round and then advanced to the final. His performance cemented a remarkable comeback.

The Tampa Bay Rays had drafted him first overall in 1999, but he battled personal issues, including drug problems. After leaving baseball for a few years, Hamilton recovered and finally made his major league debut with the Cincinnati Reds in 2007. The Reds traded the North Carolina native to the Rangers in 2008 and he led the AL in runs batted in (RBIs) that season.

Hamilton has been an All-Star in each of his first three seasons in Texas, including 2010, when he was the AL Most Valuable Player (MVP) with a league-leading .359 batting average. He also had 100 RBIs and 32 home runs despite playing in only 133 games.

Lewis and Feliz kept the Giants batters in check. The Rangers won their first World Series game by a score of 4–2.

But that was the high point of the Fall Classic for Rangers fans. The Giants' stellar pitching staff was too much for the Rangers' batters. The Giants won Games 4 and 5 to take the Series. Despite the loss, though, Rangers fans rejoiced.

"Typical of the many milestones this team achieved in this best of seasons, the Rangers managed to lose almost without disappointment," an editorial in the *Dallas Morning News* stated, "to inspire hundreds of thousands of fans—long suffering and newcomers—even in defeat."

Outfielder Josh Hamilton was named an All-Star in each of his first three seasons with the Rangers, from 2008 to 2010.

WINNING THE PENNANT

CHAPTER 2

SAME OLD SENATORS

Major League Baseball (MLB) decided to add two expansion teams to the AL following the 1960 season. One team was awarded to Anaheim, California. That team became the Angels. As for the second new team? The league had little choice.

Calvin Griffith had owned a team in Washington DC called the Senators. They had been playing there since 1901. But in October 1960, he moved the club to Minnesota. They became the Twins.

The actual United States senators—and other powerful people in Washington—were furious. They threatened to sue MLB if the city did not get another team. So on October 26, 1960, the league awarded a new team to the nation's capital. The new team was also called the Senators.

The new Senators had something else in common with the old Senators: they lost a lot of games. The old Senators had gone 27 straight seasons

Senators outfielder/first baseman Frank Howard was an All-Star every year from 1968 to 1971. He led the AL in home runs in 1968 and 1970.

SAME OLD SENATORS 13

The legendary Ted Williams, *left*, became manager of the Senators in 1969. He managed pitcher Denny McLain, *right*, in 1971.

without reaching the postseason. The new Senators failed to qualify for the postseason during their 11 seasons in Washington. They had losing records 10 times and lost 100 or more games four times.

The new Senators franchise had a typical start for an expansion team. The 1961 Senators featured few good players and finished 61–100. The team lost at least 100 games in each of the next three seasons, too. Washington DC and the Senators became the butt of a popular joke: "First in war, first in peace, and last in the American League."

However, the Senators of the late 1960s became more respectable. Outfielder Frank Howard was one of baseball's top sluggers. First baseman

> ## Frank Howard
>
> Nicknamed "Hondo" and "The Capital Punisher," the 6-foot-7, 255-pound Frank Howard was the lone star during the Senators' 11 years in Washington. A first baseman and outfielder, Howard smashed more than 40 home runs and drove in more than 100 runs for three straight seasons from 1968 to 1970. His 246 homers with Washington and Texas are the third most in club history. He was an All-Star each year from 1968 to 1971.

Mike Epstein twice had more than 20 homers in a season. Former Senators All-Star pitcher Camilo Pascual returned to Washington to post consecutive 12- and 13-win seasons. The Senators also moved into a brand-new stadium in 1962. It was later renamed RFK Stadium.

The Senators had their best season in 1969, when they won 86 games. Legendary Boston Red Sox outfielder Ted Williams became the team's manager that season. Howard smacked 48 homers, drove in 111 runs, and finished fourth in voting for the AL MVP Award. Dick Bosman won 14 games and led the AL with a 2.19 earned-run average (ERA). Williams was named AL Manager of the Year.

"My most memorable year [in Washington] was 1969," Howard said later. "We won 86 games. For our club, that was like winning the World Series."

Seasons like 1969 were rare, however. In fact, that was their only winning season in Washington. Losing did not sit well with new owner Bob Short. He had spent a lot of money trying to improve the team since buying it in 1968, but with mixed results. He continued spending money after the Senators sank back down to 70–92 in 1970. However, his strategy backfired.

The Senators traded for pitcher Denny McLain and outfielder Curt Flood before the 1971 season. Both were former All-Stars. But they contributed to a disaster in 1971. Flood left the team without warning in April. McLain lost 22 games. Howard was the only player on the team to hit more than 10 homers. The starting second baseman, Tim Cullen, hit .191. Starting shortstop Toby Harrah hit .230.

The season had barely begun when it became clear that the Senators were well on their way to another losing season. Short was losing a lot of money. So he threatened to move the team.

Few took Short seriously at first. The Senators were in the middle of the pack in attendance despite charging high ticket prices. They earned above-average revenues for broadcasting their games in Washington. Even Short credited fans for their strong support.

"You get 800,000 people to pay our prices to see our team in that stadium and you've gotta believe they're dedicated," he said in August.

"Do they deserve to be deserted?" a *Sports Illustrated* writer wondered. "Baseball wouldn't dare."

Bob Short

Bob Short was most responsible for the Dallas-Fort Worth area getting its major league team. Short owned the Washington Senators and Texas Rangers from 1968 to 1974. He moved the franchise to Texas after the 1971 season. A former treasurer for the Democratic National Committee, the Minnesota native had owned the National Basketball Association's Lakers from 1957 to 1965. He purchased the Senators on December 3, 1968. Short sold the Rangers to a group led by Brad Corbett in May 1974.

A Senators fan leans over the dugout to shake hands with Dave Nelson in the ninth inning of the Senators' farewell appearance at RFK Stadium in 1971.

Baseball did dare, though. In September, Short persuaded the other MLB owners to allow him to move the Senators from Washington again. He chose the Dallas-Fort Worth area as their new home.

The Senators played their last game in Washington on September 30, 1971. With the Senators leading the Yankees 7–5 in the ninth inning, fans streamed out onto the field. They tried to grab any souvenir that they could. Umpires failed to get the mob under control and halted the game. The Senators forfeited to the Yankees.

Short, Williams, and many of the players made the move to Texas. Before they got there, they adopted a new name: the Rangers.

CHAPTER 3
NEW HOME ON THE RANGE

Major League Baseball debuted in the Dallas-Fort Worth area on April 21, 1972. The Texas Rangers hosted the California Angels in front of 20,105 fans at Arlington Stadium. Rangers slugger Frank Howard crushed a home run and shortstop Toby Harrah smacked three hits as the Rangers won 7–6.

Sports Illustrated captured the scene: "As the Rangers were introduced, no great football roar went up from the crowd of 20,105. There was only the light clattering sound of clapping. It was a baseball crowd all right, and a dignified one. . . . Baseball truly needs a place like Dallas-Fort Worth."

Dallas-Fort Worth, however, did not need baseball. Football ruled in north Texas during the 1970s. The National Football League's Dallas Cowboys were winning Super

After a slow start in their new home, the Rangers had something to cheer about when Jeff Burroughs was named the AL MVP in 1974.

Ferguson Jenkins had a franchise-record 25 wins in 1974. He pitched for the Rangers in 1974 and 1975 and again from 1978 to 1981.

Bowls. College and high school football teams were very popular as well.

The area did not warm up to the Rangers. It did not help that the Rangers played in a

20   TEXAS RANGERS

> ### Charlie Hough
>
> Charlie Hough won 139 games and struck out 1,452 batters while pitching for the Rangers from 1980 to 1990. The knuckleballer holds franchise records in both categories. Born in Hawaii and raised in Florida, Hough was drafted by the Los Angeles Dodgers in 1966 and sold to the Rangers in 1980. He led the AL in complete games with 17 in 1984. He retired with 216 wins and 2,362 strikeouts.

converted minor league ballpark, often in the intense Texas summer heat. It also hurt that the Rangers rarely won. The first Rangers squad lost 100 games. The second Rangers squad lost 105. The team never made the playoffs between 1972 and 1995. Half of those seasons ended with losing records. Six of them ended with more than 90 losses.

The Rangers of the 1970s, 1980s, and early 1990s featured some good players and good managers. They sometimes challenged for the AL West Division crown. But they never achieved much.

The team hired Billy Martin as manager in 1973. Martin had led the Minnesota Twins and Detroit Tigers to division titles. He was a fiery manager who understood the game. And he quickly turned the Rangers around. They won 84 games in 1974 and enjoyed their first pennant race before fading in September.

The Rangers hovered around .500 in 1975 and 1976, however, and Martin was fired. The Rangers won 94 games in 1977. They also finished above .500 in three of the next four seasons. Led by homegrown standouts such as infielder Harrah, first baseman Mike Hargrove, and catcher Jim Sundberg, the Rangers were regular playoff contenders.

Nolan Ryan gets carried off the field by his teammates in 1991 after throwing his seventh career no-hitter.

Those teams, however, never made the playoffs. Neither did any of the Rangers teams of the 1980s. They lost at least 90 games in 1982, 1984, and 1985. The Rangers gambled on veteran players who did not turn out. Meanwhile, they traded away many good prospects such as pitchers Dave Righetti, Ron Darling, Walt Terrell, and Tom Henke.

Ruben Sierra

Ruben Sierra was a standout outfielder for the Rangers from 1986 to 1992, 2000 to 2001, and in 2003. He is fifth in franchise history with 1,281 hits, 180 homers, and 742 RBIs. Nicknamed "El Caballo" (The Horse), Sierra led the AL in triples, RBIs, and total bases in 1989.

In 1984 the Rangers hired new leadership. At age 36, general manager Tom Grieve was the youngest general manager in the majors. The next year he hired Bobby Valentine, 35, making him the youngest manager.

"I had no revolutionary ideas," Grieve said. "I just knew what successful organizations did. I could look at Toronto or the Mets or Cincinnati and see that they poured their time, money, and energy into scouting and development."

Grieve and Valentine rebuilt the Rangers. Their young squad surprisingly contended for the division title in 1986. They continued to build with young players in 1987 and 1988.

Then the Rangers really made moves. A group led by George W. Bush bought the team. Bush's father was the

RYAN EXPRESS

Texas native Nolan Ryan pitched for the Rangers from 1989 to 1993 and became the first player to enter the Baseball Hall of Fame wearing a Rangers cap. He played an MLB-record 27 seasons and finished with a record 5,714 career strikeouts. While with the Rangers, the right-hander notched his 5,000th career strikeout in 1989, earned his 300th victory in 1990, and tossed two no-hitters. He is the oldest pitcher to throw a no-hitter. Nicknamed "Ryan Express," his fastball topped out around 100 miles per hour.

"Ryan may be the greatest physical specimen ever to pitch," *Newsweek* magazine wrote in 1989. "Not only has he pitched at the highest level of the sport, but he's also done it for a long time."

Ryan returned as the Rangers' president in 2008. He helped put together the team that won the 2010 pennant. He also was part of a group that bought the team in 2010.

president of the United States at the time, and Bush later became president himself. On the field, Grieve traded for starting pitcher Jamie Moyer, first baseman Rafael Palmeiro, and second baseman Julio Franco. He also signed starting pitcher Nolan Ryan. Ryan was a Texas native who was headed for the Hall of Fame. The 1989 Rangers burst out to a 17–5 start and were still contending in the AL West in July.

"I go back a long time, longer than anybody, and I have never seen anything like this," Sundberg said. "Something is happening here."

"The people running the baseball side are developing a lot of good young players," said pitcher Charlie Hough. "These guys have done a great job."

The Rangers finished 83–79. However, that was 16 games behind the Oakland Athletics in the AL West. The A's eventually won the World Series. The Rangers posted an identical record the next season. This time they finished 20 games behind the A's.

Not even a 14-game winning streak in May and the highest-scoring lineup in baseball could help them win the division in 1991. Valentine was fired after the Rangers struggled in 1992. Yet they did not improve much.

The Streak

The Rangers won a team-record 14 straight games in May 1991. They tied the 1988 Oakland Athletics with the longest win streak since 1980. During that hot stretch, the Rangers scored at least five runs in every game. They averaged eight runs per game and outscored opponents by four runs per game. The streak gave the Rangers a one-game lead over the Athletics in the AL West. That was the first time the Rangers had led the division in five years.

As of 2010, outfielder Ruben Sierra sat fifth in Rangers franchise history in hits (1,281), homers (180), and RBIs (742).

The Rangers of the late 1980s and early 1990s had fundamental problems. They had power hitters such as Palmeiro, catcher Ivan Rodriguez, and outfielders Juan Gonzalez and Ruben Sierra. They also had power pitchers such as Ryan and Bobby Witt. But they played poor defense, lacked a good closer, and made too many errors running the bases.

A new generation in Rangers baseball began in 1994. After playing in a stadium that was originally built for a minor league team for their first 22 years in Texas, the Rangers

NEW HOME ON THE RANGE 25

moved into The Ballpark at Arlington. With seating for 49,292 and an old-time feel, it was instantly considered one of the finest stadiums in the majors.

"We feel we're going to be one of the next great sports franchises," team president Tom Schieffer said.

The 1994 Rangers were atop the AL West when the season was cut short due to a players' strike after 114 games. However, they only had a 52–62 record.

The team overhauled its leadership again after the season. Doug Melvin became general manager. He hired Johnny Oates as manager. Melvin and Oates had helped the Baltimore Orioles go from 107 losses in 1988 to contenders from 1992 to 1994. They would soon help bring the Rangers into their first era of winning.

Perfection

Left-handed pitcher Kenny Rogers threw the 14th perfect game in MLB history when the Rangers beat the California Angels 4–0 on July 28, 1994, in Texas. Rogers struck out eight and threw 64 of 98 pitches for strikes. He retired Angels shortstop Gary DiSarcina on a fly to center for the final out. It was the first perfect game in franchise history. Rogers won 133 games while pitching for the Rangers from 1989 to 1995, 2000 to 2002, and 2004 to 2005.

The Ballpark at Arlington set the standard for new stadiums when it debuted in 1994.

NEW HOME ON THE RANGE

CHAPTER 4

A NEW ERA

Although the Rangers had hired a new general manager and a new manager before the 1995 season, they added few impact players. Manager Johnny Oates and general manager Doug Melvin instead sought to tweak the team they had. They focused on improving the defense, pitching, base running, and the clubhouse atmosphere.

The Rangers already had a powerful lineup. Young stars such as catcher Ivan Rodriguez, designated hitter/outfielder Juan Gonzalez, third baseman Dean Palmer, and outfielder Rusty Greer combined with veteran first baseman Will Clark to give the team a formidable batting order. They also had a staff ace in Kenny Rogers.

The team added role players such as second baseman Mark McLemore and outfielder Otis Nixon as well as utility player Mickey Tettleton. They also reacquired pitcher Bobby Witt and signed starter Kevin Gross.

Outfielder Juan Gonzalez won the AL MVP Award in 1996 and 1998 while with the Rangers.

Dean Palmer, *center*, is congratulated by teammates Ivan Rodriguez, *left*, Mickey Tettleton, and Will Clark, *right*, after hitting a grand slam in 1996.

The team also let go of some veterans who had bad attitudes.

The moves set the tone for a new era of Rangers baseball. It was the team's first period of sustained success.

In 1995, the Rangers stood in first place in mid-July before eventually falling to third in the AL West. But they built on that success in 1996. Led by stars such as Gonzalez, Rodriguez,

> ### Series-less
>
> After the 2010 season, the Rangers were one of only eight teams to have never won a World Series. At 50 seasons, the Rangers had the longest drought of the eight teams. That was one year longer than the Houston Astros. The other teams on the list include the Colorado Rockies, the Milwaukee Brewers, the San Diego Padres, the Seattle Mariners, the Tampa Bay Rays, and the Washington Nationals.

Palmer, and ace Ken Hill, the Rangers won their first seven games and were 33–19 on May 29. That marked the first time the Rangers were 14 games over .500 in 17 years.

Even another late-season swoon could not stop them. After losing nine of 10 games, the Rangers' lead was reduced to one game over the Seattle Mariners on September 20. But the Rangers then won four of five. On September 27, when the Mariners lost to the Oakland Athletics, the Rangers clinched their first division title. Gonzalez was the AL MVP.

"By winning, we put all that [bad history] behind us," team president Tom Schieffer said. "This is confirmation that things have changed, that we're not a sad-sack franchise anymore."

The Rangers won their first game in the ALDS against the New York Yankees, too. Gonzalez and Palmer blasted home runs. Starter John Burkett struck out seven in a complete game as the Rangers won 6–2. However, things fell apart after that. The Rangers were five outs away from winning Game 2 when the Yankees tied it up. The Yankees eventually won in the 12th inning.

Game 3 was the first playoff game ever in Dallas-Fort Worth. The Rangers built a 2–1 lead on a Gonzalez home run

A NEW ERA **31**

GONZO

Juan Gonzalez homered in all four games of the 1996 ALDS against the New York Yankees. He is one of only two players in major league history to homer in four straight playoff games. Gonzalez hit a total of five homers in the series while batting .438 with nine RBIs.

"Juan had a tremendous series," Yankees designated hitter Cecil Fielder said. "It seems like every time he came up we just kept getting the ball right in the middle of his bat."

Gonzalez smacked 372 home runs while playing in Texas from 1989 to 1999 and 2002 to 2003. Nicknamed "Juan Gone," he ranks first in Rangers history in homers and RBIs (1,180) and fourth in hits (1,595). The Puerto Rico native was named the AL MVP in 1996 and 1998, led the AL in homers in 1992 and 1993, and led the AL in RBIs in 1998.

and an RBI double by Rodriguez. But the Yankees scored twice in the ninth to win the game 3–2. The Rangers again held a lead in Game 4. But the Yankees made up a four-run deficit and eventually won 6–4.

The difference in the series was the bullpens. The Rangers scored 16 runs in the series, but none after the sixth inning. The Yankees, meanwhile, scored seven runs after the sixth.

After falling back to 77–85 in 1997, the Rangers were back in the playoff hunt in 1998. The Rangers and California Angels were tied with seven games to play when they met for a three-game series in Anaheim. The Rangers swept the series. Greer and Gonzalez had monster games and the Rangers' starters pitched well as Texas

Rusty Greer helped the Rangers with his glove and bat during their run to the 1998 West Division title.

outscored the Angels by a combined 25–3. The Rangers won the division and returned to the playoffs. However, the Yankees swept them in the ALDS.

The 1999 Rangers were perhaps the best in franchise history to that point. They won 95 games—the most in team history—and again won the AL West. Six Rangers hit at least 20 homers. Rodriguez, Gonzalez, and designated hitter Rafael Palmeiro each hit more

Perfect in the Field

How good was the Rangers defense in 1996? They set a major league record by playing 15 consecutive games without committing an error. However, that record has since been surpassed by the 2007 Boston Red Sox (17) and the 2009 New York Yankees (19).

than 35 home runs, drove in more than 110 runs, and hit over .320. Rodriguez was the AL MVP. Closer John Wetteland saved 43 games. However, the team's starting pitching struggled, and the Rangers had poor defense.

The Rangers' flaws always caught up with them in the postseason. The Yankees again swept the Rangers in the ALDS.

Although the Rangers had been competitive in the 1996 playoffs, they were not in 1998 or 1999. Texas scored a total of one run in both the 1998 and 1999 playoffs.

"With our offense, our ball club, to me it's mind-boggling," Oates said during the 1999 ALDS. "Just by accident, we should score some runs."

After waiting so long to reach the postseason, the Rangers made it three times in the late 1990s. But by the time the decade ended, the frustration was with failing to win in the postseason. However, as the Rangers struggled into the twenty-first century, their fans came to appreciate that those Rangers teams had played some of the best baseball in the franchise's history.

Pudge

Ivan "Pudge" Rodriguez was a top defensive catcher and an elite hitter with the Rangers from 1991 to 2002 and in 2009. He ranks second in team history in hits (1,747), fourth in homers (217), and third in RBIs (842). He was named the 1999 AL MVP and won a Gold Glove every year from 1992 to 2001. The Puerto Rico native has played more games at catcher than anyone in MLB history.

Juan Gonzalez celebrates the Rangers' third AL West Division title in four years in 1999.

A NEW ERA

CHAPTER 5

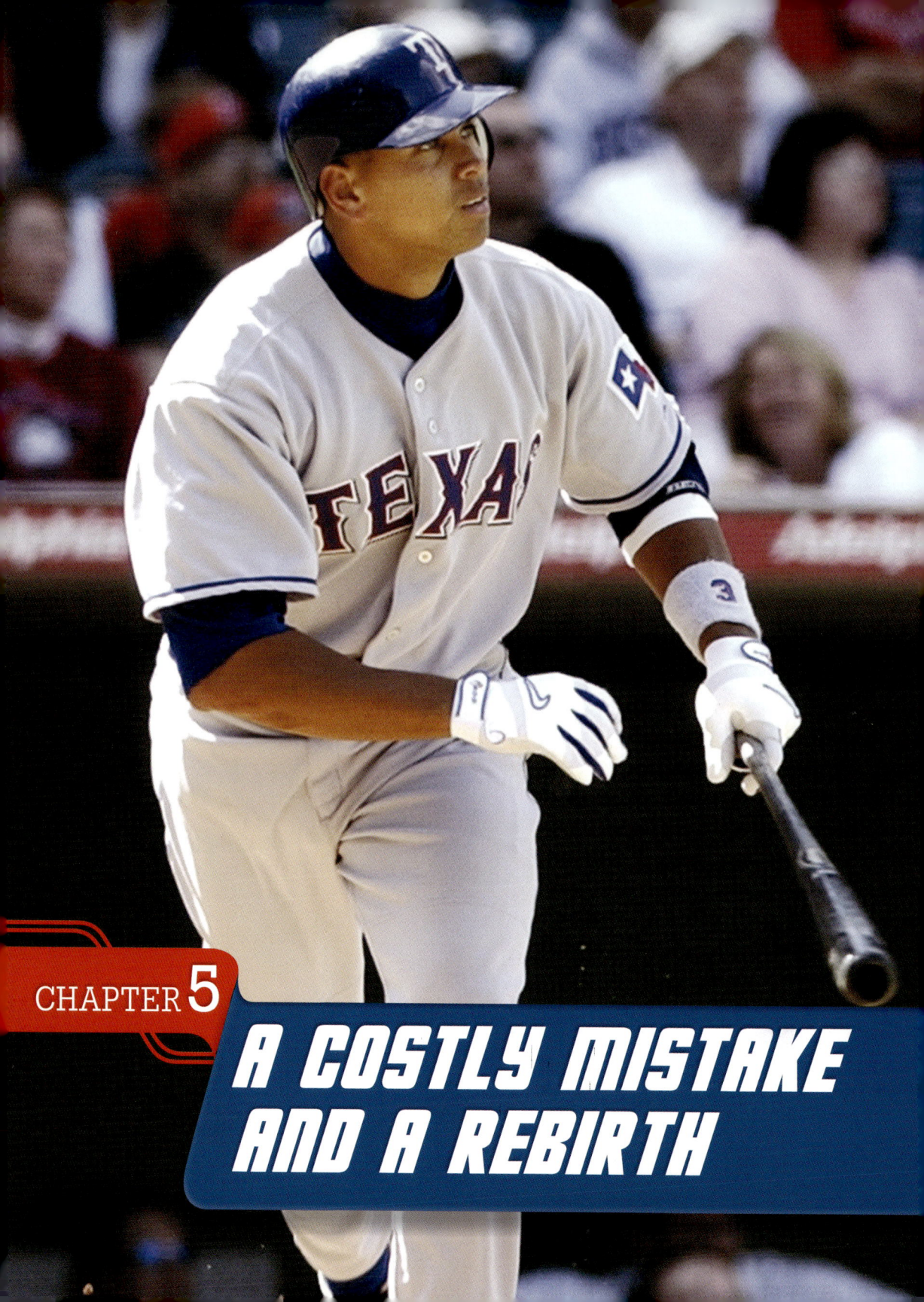

A COSTLY MISTAKE AND A REBIRTH

On December 11, 2000, All-Star shortstop Alex Rodriguez signed a 10-year, $252 million contract to play for the Rangers. It was the largest contract in MLB history. And with that, one of the most frustrating eras in Rangers history began.

Signing Rodriguez seemed like a good idea at the time. The 25-year-old finished third in the AL MVP voting in 2000. Although the Rangers had lost 91 games in 2000, they had some star players, such as catcher Ivan Rodriguez, first baseman Rafael Palmeiro, and left fielder Rusty Greer.

"We get a couple of more players, and we can win this thing," pitcher Kenny Rogers said. "I don't know if we have enough pitching, but I know, with all these new guys, that we have enough hitting."

Rogers's fear was correct. The Rangers did not need more offense. They needed pitching.

Alex Rodriguez became the youngest player to hit 300 home runs when he reached the milestone on April 2, 2003.

A COSTLY MISTAKE AND A REBIRTH   37

THE BIG DEAL

Not everybody agreed that it was smart of the Rangers to award Alex Rodriguez the richest contract in baseball history in 2000.

"The Texas Rangers just made what may be the most stupid decision in the history of American professional sport," wrote one newspaper columnist. "They talk themselves into thinking that Rodriguez ... is a unique player worth any amount of money. He's not ... While Rodriguez, 25, is a probable Hall of Famer, he isn't remotely close to being a man who can produce a championship by himself."

The critics were correct. A-Rod led the league in homers during all three seasons in Texas and was named the 2003 AL MVP. But Texas never posted a winning record while he was there. His image was further tarnished after he left the Rangers when Rodriguez admitted to taking illegal performance enhancing drugs while with the Rangers.

In 2000, the Rangers' 5.52 ERA was the worst in the majors. They did not add any impact starters in 2001. Meanwhile, closer John Wetteland retired.

Alex Rodriguez produced just as expected. He averaged a .305 batting average, 52 homers, and 132 RBIs in his three seasons with the Rangers. He also won Gold Gloves in 2002 and 2003 and was the 2003 AL MVP. Yet the Rangers lost at least 89 games in 2001, 2002, and 2003. After the 2003 season, the Rangers traded Rodriguez to the New York Yankees for second baseman Alfonso Soriano.

The trade worked at first. Texas made a surprising run in 2004. Soriano hit 28 homers and stole 18 bases. Meanwhile, homegrown stars emerged around him in the infield. First baseman Mark Teixeira, shortstop Michael Young, and

Third baseman Hank Blalock hit 32 home runs during his 2004 All-Star season.

third baseman Hank Blalock all tallied at least 20 homers and 90 RBIs. Closer Francisco Cordero saved 49 games.

With seven games to play, the Rangers were right in the thick of the AL West race. They were two games behind the Oakland A's and one back of

Michael Young

Second baseman Michael Young moved over to shortstop and filled in quite nicely when Alex Rodriguez left in 2004. He made his first of six consecutive All-Star Games that season when he hit .313 with 91 RBIs. He won the AL batting title in 2005 by hitting .331 with 221 hits and added a Gold Glove in 2008.

A COSTLY MISTAKE AND A REBIRTH 39

Rangers closer Neftali Feliz saved 40 games with a 2.73 ERA in 2010 when he was only 22 years old.

the Anaheim Angels. Then the Angels came to Texas for a four-game series. The Rangers lost the first three games despite holding leads in two of them. Although they won the fourth game, a loss in Seattle the next day eliminated the Rangers from playoff contention.

The Rangers slipped back into mediocrity. They had losing records in each of the next four seasons. But they started to show some signs of life again in 2009. The team had acquired talented outfielder Josh Hamilton in 2008. He combined with young players such as second

> ### Ian Kinsler
>
> *In 2009, second baseman Ian Kinsler became the second Texas Ranger to hit at least 30 home runs while stealing at least 30 bases. The Arizona native has been a key batter in the Rangers lineup since joining the big-league club in 2006. He was named an All-Star in 2008 and 2010 and stole at least 20 bases from 2007 to 2009. Injuries slowed him down a bit in 2010, but the former University of Missouri star was key in the postseason. He hit three homers and had nine RBIs.*

baseman Ian Kinsler and outfielder Nelson Cruz, as well as veterans such as Young, to turn the Rangers back into a winning team.

The Rangers got off to a 30–19 start. They led the division as late as July 10. A five-game losing streak in mid-September almost buried them. But the Rangers still stood a chance as the season's final week began. However, they lost a game at home to the Tampa Bay Rays and then lost three games on the road against the Angels to ensure they would miss the playoffs for the tenth straight year.

It was a disappointing finish, but the foundation had been set for the team that would go on to win the 2010 AL pennant. In 2010, Hamilton cemented himself as one of the top batters in all of baseball by winning the AL MVP Award.

Others, such as Kinsler, Cruz, and Young, helped give Texas one of the AL's top batting orders. Meanwhile, young pitchers such as Tommy Hunter and closer Neftali Feliz gave Rangers fans hope that the team had finally shed its recent reputation for weak pitching.

With those players leading the way, the Rangers hope to show that they can remain a winning franchise for a long time.

TIMELINE

1960 — The Rangers are born as the Washington Senators, an expansion team in the AL, on October 26. They begin play in 1961.

1971 — The other MLB owners approve Senators owner Bob Short's request to move the Senators to Texas.

1972 — The Texas Rangers play their first game, losing 1–0 on the road against the California Angels on April 15. The Rangers defeat the Angels 5–1 on April 16 for the first victory in club history.

1974 — The Rangers enjoy a breakout season, finishing just five games out of first in the AL West. Manager Billy Martin is named AL Manager of the Year, first baseman Mike Hargrove is named AL Rookie of the Year, and right fielder Jeff Burroughs is named AL MVP.

1985 — The Rangers hire Bobby Valentine as manager on May 16. He leads the Rangers until 1992.

1989 — Rangers pitcher Nolan Ryan fans Oakland Athletics outfielder Rickey Henderson on August 22 for his 5,000th career strikeout. He is the first pitcher in baseball history with 5,000 strikeouts.

1990 — Ryan beats the Milwaukee Brewers 11–3 on July 31 to earn his 300th career win.

1991 — Ryan no-hits the Toronto Blue Jays in a 3–0 win on May 1. It is Ryan's seventh career no-hitter, the most in baseball history. At 44, he also becomes the oldest pitcher in history to toss a no-hitter.

42 TEXAS RANGERS

1994	The Rangers lose 4–3 to the Brewers on April 11 in the first game at their new stadium, The Ballpark in Arlington.
1996	When the Seattle Mariners lose to the Athletics on September 27, the Rangers clinch the AL West Division. It is the franchise's first division title.
1996	The Rangers defeat the New York Yankees 6–2 in Game 1 of the ALDS on October 1 for the first postseason win in franchise history.
1996	Rangers manager Johnny Oates is named AL Manager of the Year and outfielder Juan Gonzalez is named AL MVP.
1999	Ryan becomes the first player to be inducted into the Baseball Hall of Fame wearing a Rangers cap on his plaque.
1999	Rangers catcher Ivan Rodriguez is named AL MVP. The Rangers win a division title for the third time in four years. But also for the third time in four years, they lose to the Yankees in the ALDS.
2000	Shortstop Alex Rodriguez signs a $252 million contract with the Rangers on December 11. It is the largest contract in MLB history.
2008	Ryan is named the Rangers' club president.
2010	The Rangers finish 90–72 and win the AL West Division. They beat the Tampa Bay Rays in the ALDS to win their first postseason series ever and then beat the Yankees in the ALCS before losing to the San Francisco Giants in the franchise's first World Series.

QUICK STATS

FRANCHISE HISTORY
Washington Senators (1961–71)
Texas Rangers (1972–)

WORLD SERIES
(wins in bold)
2010

AL CHAMPIONSHIP SERIES
(1969–)
2010

DIVISION CHAMPIONSHIPS
(1969–)
1996, 1998, 1999, 2010

KEY PLAYERS
(position[s]; seasons with team)
Juan Gonzalez (OF; 1989–99, 2002–03)
Rusty Greer (OF; 1994–2002)
Josh Hamilton (OF; 2008–)
Charlie Hough (SP; 1980–90)
Frank Howard (OF/1B; 1965–72)
Ferguson Jenkins (SP; 1974–75, 1978–81)
Dean Palmer (3B; 1989, 1991–97)
Ivan Rodriguez (C; 1991–2002, 2009)
Kenny Rogers (SP; 1989–95, 2000–02, 2004–05)
Nolan Ryan (SP; 1989–93)
Ruben Sierra (OF; 1986–92, 2000–01, 2003)
Jim Sundberg (C; 1974–83, 1988–89)
Michael Young (SS/2B/3B; 2000–)

KEY MANAGERS
Johnny Oates (1995–2001): 506–476; 1–9 (postseason)
Ron Washington (2007–) 331–317; 8–8 (postseason)

HOME PARKS
Griffith Stadium (1961)
D.C. Stadium/RFK Stadium (1962–71)
Arlington Stadium (1972–93)
Rangers Ballpark in Arlington (1994–)
   Known as The Ballpark at Arlington (1994–2004), Ameriquest Field (2005–06)

* All statistics through 2010 season

44   TEXAS RANGERS

QUOTES AND ANECDOTES

Arlington Stadium, where the Rangers played from 1972 to 1993, was known as one of the worst stadiums in the majors. It was built in 1965 as a minor league ballpark called Turnpike Stadium. Although it expanded to a 43,000-seat ballpark when the Rangers moved to Texas, according to former team president Tom Schieffer, it was still "a minor-league facility in every way."

Four men managed the Rangers during an eight-day span in 1977. They were Frank Lucchesi, Eddie Stanky, Connie Ryan, and Billy Hunter. Lucchesi was fired midway through the season and replaced by Stanky. He managed one game and resigned. Ryan was named interim manager and lasted six games. Hunter then took over for good—until he was fired in 1978. All told, the Rangers employed 13 managers during their first 14 seasons in Texas.

"We had a unique kind of pressure this year. Since the All-Star break we've heard a lot about how the Rangers always collapse. I was looking over my shoulder, but not at the Mariners, at history. I have all the respect in the world for the Mariners, A's, and Angels, but the biggest obstacle we've had to overcome was our history."—Rangers manager Johnny Oates, on how his team overcame a major obstacle to win the first division title in franchise history in 1996.

"The entire pitching staff had a total of three complete major league games among them in 1960. The starting outfield could scrape together a record of 22 home runs, and the infielders were known, if at all, as players who could neither field nor hit."—*Sports Illustrated*, describing the new Senators team that debuted in 1961.

45

GLOSSARY

ace
A team's best starting pitcher.

contender
A team that is in the race for a championship or playoff berth.

designated hitter
A position used only in the American League. Managers can employ a hitter in the batting order who comes to the plate to hit instead of the pitcher.

expansion
In sports, the addition of a franchise or franchises to a league.

franchise
An entire sports organization, including the players, coaches, and staff.

general manager
The executive who is in charge of the team's overall operation. He or she hires and fires managers and coaches, drafts players, and signs free agents.

knuckleballer
A pitcher who throws a knuckleball, which is a kind of baseball pitch that has almost no spin, making it move unpredictably.

pennant
A flag. In baseball, it symbolizes that a team has won its league championship.

postseason
The games in which the best teams play after the regular-season schedule has been completed.

retire
To officially end one's career.

veteran
An individual with great experience in a particular endeavor.

wild card
Playoff berths given to the best remaining teams that did not win their respective divisions.

FOR MORE INFORMATION

Further Reading

Nadel, Eric. *The Texas Rangers: The Authorized History*. Dallas, TX: Taylor Publishing Company, 1997.

Ryan, Nolan, and Jerry B. Jenkins. *Miracle Man: Nolan Ryan, the Autobiography*. Dallas, TX: Thomas Nelson Publishers, 2004.

Vecsey, George. *Baseball: A History of America's Favorite Game*. New York: Modern Library, 2008.

Web Links

To learn more about the Texas Rangers, visit ABDO Publishing Company online at **www.abdopublishing.com**. Web sites about the Rangers are featured on our Book Links page. These links are routinely monitored and updated to provide the most current information available.

Places to Visit

National Baseball Hall of Fame and Museum
25 Main Street
Cooperstown, NY 13326
1-888-HALL-OF-FAME
www.baseballhall.org
This hall of fame and museum highlights the greatest players and moments in the history of baseball. Former Rangers Goose Gossage, Ferguson Jenkins, Gaylord Perry, and Nolan Ryan are enshrined here.

Rangers Ballpark in Arlington
1000 Ballpark Way
Arlington, TX 76011
817-273-5222
http://texas.rangers.mlb.com/tex/ballpark/index.jsp
This has been the Rangers' home field since 1994. Tours are available when the Rangers are not playing.

Surprise Stadium
15754 North Bullard
Surprise, AZ 85374
623-266-8100
http://texas.rangers.mlb.com/spring_training/ballpark.jsp?c_id=tex
Surprise Stadium has been the Rangers' spring-training ballpark since 2002.

INDEX

Arlington Stadium, 19

Ballpark at Arlington, The. *See* Rangers Ballpark in Arlington
Blalock, Hank, 39
Burkett, John, 31
Bush, George W. (owner), 23–24

Cantu, Jorge, 7
Clark, Will, 29
Corbett, Brad, 16
Cruz, Nelson, 6, 8, 41
Cullen, Tim, 16

Darling, Ron, 22

Epstein, Mike, 15

Feliz, Neftali, 5, 6, 9, 10, 41
Flood, Curt, 16
Franco, Julio, 24

Gonzalez, Juan, 25, 29, 30, 31, 32, 33
Greer, Rusty, 29, 32, 37
Grieve, Tom (general manager), 23–24
Gross, Kevin, 29
Guerrero, Vladimir, 8

Hamilton, Josh, 6, 10, 40, 41
Hargrove, Mike, 21
Harrah, Toby, 16, 19, 21
Henke, Tom, 22
Hill, Ken, 31
Hough, Charlie, 21, 24
Howard, Frank, 14, 15, 16, 19
Hunter, Tommy, 41

Kinsler, Ian, 6, 8, 41

Lee, Cliff, 6, 7, 8
Lewis, Colby, 8, 10

Martin, Billy (manager), 21
McLain, Denny, 16
McLemore, Mark, 29
Melvin, Doug (general manager), 26, 29
Moreland, Mitch, 9
Moyer, Jamie, 24

Nixon, Otis, 29

Oates, Johnny (manager), 26, 29, 34
O'Day, Darren, 7
Oliver, Darren, 7

Palmeiro, Rafael, 24, 25, 33, 37
Palmer, Dean, 29, 31
Pascual, Camilo, 15

Rangers Ballpark in Arlington, 5, 26
RFK Stadium, 15
Righetti, Dave, 22
Rodriguez, Alex, 5, 37, 38, 39
Rodriguez, Ivan, 25, 29, 30, 32, 33, 34, 37
Rogers, Kenny, 26, 29, 37
Ryan, Nolan (player, owner, and president), 23, 24, 25

Schieffer, Tom (president), 26, 31
Short, Bob (owner), 15, 16–17
Sierra, Ruben, 22, 25
Soriano, Alfonso, 38
Sundberg, Jim, 21, 24

Teixeira, Mark, 38
Terrell, Walt, 22
Tettleton, Mickey, 29

Valentine, Bobby (manager), 23, 24

Washington, Ron (manager), 6
Wetteland, John, 34, 38
Williams, Ted (manager), 15, 17
Wilson, C. J., 7, 8
Witt, Bobby, 25, 29
World Series, 5, 9–10

Young, Michael, 6, 8, 38, 39, 41

About the Author

Ryan Basen is a writer and journalism professor living in Charlotte, North Carolina. He grew up in the Washington DC area. A former newspaper and magazine reporter, Basen has also written books about several sports. He earned awards from the N.C. Press Association and Associated Press Sports Editors for work he did as a reporter with the *Charlotte Observer* newspaper in 2007 and 2008.

TICKET, Please

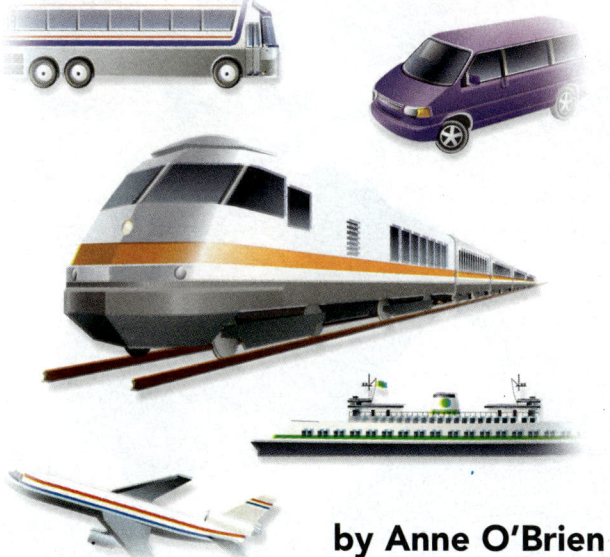

by Anne O'Brien

Harcourt

Orlando Boston Dallas Chicago San Diego

Visit *The Learning Site!*
www.harcourtschool.com

Imagine that you are taking a vacation trip with your parents. How will you get there? What kind of transportation will you take? You might drive in a car.

In a car, you can choose the roads you want to drive on. You can drive on a big highway or a small country road. You can stop wherever you like. You can visit people or places along the way. If you get hungry, you can find a restaurant along the way.

You might take a bus on your trip. Buses travel to almost every town in America. You can buy your ticket at the bus station. You can check the timetable to see what time the bus leaves.

The bus travels by highway from one town to the next. You can look out the window and watch the country go by. You can talk to your family. You can listen to your favorite music on headphones. When you get tired, you can take a nap in your seat.

You might take a train on your trip. You can buy a ticket at the train station. The train station bustles with people coming and going from many different places. You can take a train to the next town or all the way across the country.

On the train, the conductor will punch your ticket. As the train speeds along, you can read books or play games. When you're hungry, you can walk through the train to the dining car for a snack. Some trains even have beds for sleeping!

You might take an airplane on your trip. Jet planes are the fastest way to travel. Airplanes can take you to another country in just a few hours. When you arrive at the airport, you check your suitcase. You show your ticket and you get a special pass that allows you to walk on the plane.

When everyone has boarded, the plane moves down the runway. It builds up speed and lifts into the air. From high in the sky, you can see for miles around. Everything on the ground looks tiny. As the plane flies through the air, you can watch a movie and eat a meal or two.

If you are going to an island, you might take a ferry. The ferry travels from the mainland to the island. Some ferries take only passengers. Other ferries also take cars. You can drive your car right onto the boat!

Some people take ferries to work everyday. Other people take long overnight ferry rides from one country to another. A ferry is like a bus on the water. You can sit inside and stay dry. You can also stand on the deck and feel the sea breeze as you sail across the bay.

Once you get to the place you are visiting, there are many ways to get around. What form of transportation will you choose? Walking is a great way to meet people and see the sights. If you are near a park, you might hike on a trail in the woods.

You might take bicycles to get around. In many places, you can rent bicycles to ride. You can see the sights and get exercise, too. Some places have special bike paths to keep bikers safe from cars.

If you are in a city, you might take a taxicab to get around. A taxicab is a special kind of car with a driver. The taxi driver takes passengers where they want to go. You pay the driver when the trip is over.

If you are in a big city, you might take the subway to get around. A subway is a train that runs under the ground. You walk down stairs until you are below the street. City people take the subway to work everyday. You can also take it to a museum or to a zoo.

When you go on your vacation trip, there are so many kinds of transportation you can take. What kind of travel will you choose?